WILD RIVER

WILD RIVER

p. j. petersen

a yearling book

All rights reserved. Published in the United States by Yearling, an imprint of Random House Children's Books, a division of Random House, Inc., New York. Originally published in hardcover in the United States by Delacorte Press, an imprint of Random House Children's Books, New York, in 2009.

Yearling and the jumping horse design are registered trademarks of Random House, Inc.

Visit us on the Web! randomhouse.com/kids

Educators and librarians, for a variety of teaching tools, visit us at RHTeachersLibrarians.com

The Library of Congress has cataloged the hardcover edition of this work as follows:
Petersen, P. J.
Wild river / P. J. Petersen. — 1st ed.
p. cm.
Summary: Considered lazy and unathletic, twelve-year-old Ryan discovers a heroic side of himself when a kayak trip with his older brother goes horribly awry.
ISBN 978-0-385-73724-1 (hardcover) — ISBN 978-0-385-90656-2 (lib. bdg.) — ISBN 978-0-375-89268-4 (ebook)
[1. Wilderness survival—Fiction. 2. Survival—Fiction. 3. Heroes—Fiction. 4. Kayaks and kayaking—Fiction. 5. Brothers—Fiction.] I. Title.
PZ7.P44197 Wj 2009
[Fic]—dc22
2008024921

ISBN 978-0-375-84624-3 (pbk.)

Printed in the United States of America

10 9 8 7 6 5 4 3 2

First Yearling Edition 2013

For my grandson,
Ryan Peter Harvey

CHAPTER ONE

The longest day of my life began with my brother, Tanner, yelling, "Wake up, Ryan. You just won a free trip."

I opened one eye and looked at the clock. Ten minutes to six. "It's the middle of the night," I said, and pulled the pillow over my head.

Tanner laughed and yanked off my blankets. "Come on. We want to get an early start. Breakfast in five minutes."

I kept the pillow on my head. "Go away."

Tanner grabbed my feet and dragged me to the edge of the bed. "Let's go, Ryan. This will be great."

I pushed away the pillow. "What's going on, Tanner?"

He flashed his big happy smile. "Brady has to work today. We got everything packed last night, and then his boss called him this morning. So I talked to Mom and Dad. And you get to come with me, little bro. Fishing, kayaking, camping. What could be better than that?"

"Lots of things," I said. "Like sleeping." But Tanner wasn't listening. He was already pulling a sweatshirt out of my dresser.

"You need warm clothes for tonight. It gets cold up there after the sun goes down." He yanked open another drawer and grabbed some jeans. "I'll stick these in the dry bag. Put on your swimsuit and a T-shirt. And wear your old tennies."

"Come on, Tanner," I said. "You can find somebody else. I'm no good at that stuff."

2

He flashed that smile again and headed for the door. "You'll do fine. Wait and see. You'll love it."

That was Tanner, my big brother. He got what he wanted. Always. He wasn't mean or bossy. He just made up his mind, and that was it. If you told him no, he didn't listen.

— — —

Mom let Tanner drive our van that morning. She was nervous about it. Tanner had only had his license for two months. But he told Mom he needed the practice. And he gave her that puppy-dog smile of his. So she said yes.

The trip to our drop-off point took more than two hours. And it seemed like two weeks. I tried to sleep, but it was hopeless. The roads were terrible—full of potholes and sharp turns. And Mom kept nagging Tanner, telling him to slow down or watch out for something. I got sick of it, and I wasn't even the one driving. But Tanner never quit smiling.

When we finally stopped, I was feeling rotten. I climbed out of the van and headed down the bank. The Boulder River didn't look big enough to be called a river. It was only about twenty feet across.

I scooped up a handful of water. It was like holding ice cubes. I dumped the water and rubbed my wet hand on my face. That woke me up.

Tanner came down and stood beside me. "We lucked out, Ryan," he said. "We really lucked out."

"Yeah, sure," I said.

"I'm serious," he said. "We lucked out."

"We're lucky I didn't puke in the van. All those stupid turns. What else?"

Tanner looked over his shoulder. "I'll tell you later. I don't want Mom to get worried."

I dipped my fingers in the water and flicked a few drops into his face. "Cold enough for you?"

Tanner laughed. "No problem. We're fishing, not swimming."

We went up the bank to the van. Mom had the tailgate open. She was shaking her head. "So much stuff."

4

"Just the right amount," Tanner said. "Brady and I made a checklist. Everything we need and not one thing more." He laughed. "Except for extra marshmallows. Brady figures you can never have too many marshmallows."

I wished Brady were there to eat them. I'd spent three years in Cub Scouts. That was enough outdoor stuff for me. I didn't like it, and I wasn't good at it. The last time Dad had taken me fishing, I'd ended up with a fishhook in my neck.

In no time Tanner had our gear laid out next to the river. He unrolled the yellow kayak. It looked like a giant balloon. Ten feet of flat plastic. I'd been kayaking with the Scouts, but I'd never been in a kayak like that.

I stood in the sun and bounced up and down to keep warm. It was one of our usual California summer days. Later on, it would be hot. But right then I needed the sweatshirt that was buried in the big rubber dry bag.

Tanner hauled out something that looked like a big bicycle pump. First he pumped up the floor of the kayak. Then he did each side. "Three sections," he told me. "Even if we spring a leak, we won't sink."

"We'd better not spring a leak," I said.

He flashed that same old smile. "We won't. But I have some patches in my pocket just in case." He was wearing shorts with big pockets. And every pocket was full.

Mom walked back and forth. "Tanner, do you have your cell?"

Tanner laughed. "We're up in the mountains, Mom. Cell phones don't work around here."

Mom reached into her purse for her phone. She fiddled with it for a minute, then put it away. "I didn't know you wouldn't have a phone."

"We have to rough it," Tanner said. "We can't even call and order a pizza."

Mom looked down at the river. "You boys be careful today."

Tanner kept pumping. "Come on, Mom. Brady and I did this last year. Nothing to it."

Mom shook her head. "Still, I can't help worrying a little."

"I know, Mom," Tanner said. "We're worried about you too. How will you and Dad get along without us tonight? With us gone, you'll probably stay up all night playing Ryan's video games. Or watching the monster movies on Channel Ten." He gave her that big smile of his.

Mom broke out laughing. "Smart aleck."

Tanner's big puppy-dog smile—it always made people smile back. They couldn't help it. The girls in his high school called him Smiley, and they were crazy about him.

Everybody liked Tanner. With good reason. He was always friendly, always kidding around. He was good at everything—school, sports, you name it. He was even a hero, with a medal from the mayor. Last spring he'd carried an old man out of a burning house.

Me? I was just Tanner's little brother. That was what everybody called me. And they always sounded a little surprised. Tanner and I didn't look much like brothers. I was four years younger. Half his size. I didn't smile as much. I wasn't that good at sports or anything else. And I sure wasn't a hero.

I was the only person who ever got mad at Tanner. He was always trying to help me. Even if I didn't want help. He thought I needed more exercise, more sports. And less video games and less time on the computer. I knew what I liked and what I didn't like. But Tanner was sure I'd be happier his way.

It was hard to stay mad at Tanner, though. He thought he was being good to me. Like that morning. He was excited about the fishing trip. So he thought I would be too. No matter what I said.

When it was pumped up, the yellow kayak looked like a giant pool toy. The sides were round and fat, like huge sausages. The front and back were pointed, with a thick sheet of plastic stretched across the top. That made a nice covered spot for my legs and feet. Except Tanner was jamming the dry bag into that space.

"Where do my feet go?" I asked.

"Lots of room, Ryan," Tanner said. "Just slide your feet on each side."

We carried the yellow kayak to the edge of the water. Tanner got out our paddles. They were aluminum with plastic blades on both ends. He fixed mine so that it was exactly my height. Then he tossed me a life vest.

"You wear that the whole time," Mom said. "You too, Tanner."

Tanner put on his life vest. Then he held the kayak while I climbed in. The kayak tipped a little. I sat down fast and jammed my feet into place, one on each side of the bag.

Right behind me was a plastic sack full of fishing gear and a coil of white rope.

"What's the rope for?" I asked.

"For the bear bag," Tanner said.

"What?"

"The bear bag. For tonight, when we're camp-ing. We'll throw the rope over a tree limb and haul our food up high so the bears can't reach it."

"Wait a minute," I said. "You didn't say anything about bears."

Tanner laughed. "Don't worry, Ryan. We'll never see a bear. We won't be that lucky."

I hoped he was right.

Before Tanner got into the kayak, Mom wanted to go over things with him one more time. Dad would pick us up at some bridge tomorrow after-noon. "Two o'clock," Tanner said. "Dad knows all about it." But Mom wrote everything down just the same.

Tanner handed me both paddles. Then he pushed the kayak into the water and climbed in. The kayak tipped to one side, then the other.

"Be careful!" I yelled.

Tanner plopped down, and his feet rammed into my back. "We're fine," he said. He took his paddle from me. "Just sit there for a minute. I'll get us started." The kayak moved out to the middle of the river. The current caught it and carried us along.

Mom shouted, "Good-bye!" and "Have a good time!" and "Be careful!" I waved my paddle but didn't look back.

"She's a little nervous," Tanner said. "She thinks this is a bad idea."

"Why'd she let us go, then?"

Tanner laughed. "She didn't want to. You should have heard her. But I told her I'd watch out for you."

"What about Dad?"

"He was no problem. I've done the trip before. And he likes the idea of you getting out and doing stuff." Tanner nudged me with his foot. "So here you are, Ryan, you lucky rat."

"Goody goody," I said.

"Just wait. By tomorrow afternoon you'll be begging me to take you again."

"You want to make a little bet on that?"

Tanner used his paddle to drip some water on my head. "Come on, Ryan. Give it a chance. Real live action for a change, not some game. It's about ten o'clock right now. Twenty-eight hours till we meet Dad. That's not very long. What do you say? For twenty-eight hours, no moaning, no worrying. Just kick back and have some fun."

"Moan, moan," I said. But I decided to try.

We didn't have to paddle hard. The current did most of the work. But there were lots of big rocks in the river, and we had to stay away from them.

I was a little scared at first. We kept missing boulders by inches. Sometimes just scraping them. I figured we'd hit one sooner or later.

Then it happened. We slid past one big boulder, and I saw another one right ahead of us. "Look out!" I yelled.

The kayak smacked the boulder hard and bounced to the right. We were sideways for a second, but then we were headed downstream again. No problem at all. I was amazed.

"See how we bounced?" Tanner said. "That's why we're using this old plastic job."

"You should have told me," I said. "I thought if

we hit a big rock, it was"—I made my voice really deep—"'Tough luck, Chuck. Heh-heh-heh.'"

"'Tough luck, Chuck'? Where'd that come from?"

"This video game I was playing last night. Chopper Demon. It's a motorcycle race. You go roaring along, making jumps and zapping bad guys. Then this skeleton on a giant motorcycle—Chopper Demon—comes along and wipes you out. And he yells things like 'Eat dirt, Squirt!' and lets out this rotten laugh: 'Heh-heh-heh.'"

Tanner laughed. "'Eat dirt, Squirt.' I like that. How long did it take you to beat him?"

"I just got the game yesterday. Kenny let me borrow it. He hates it. Says he's tired of losing and getting laughed at."

"What about you?"

"I'm working on it. I was up till midnight last night. You have to go after the Demon early in the game. Mess up his tires and his gas. But he's tricky. I'm still getting crunched most of the time."

"If you worked half that hard—" he started.

"You sound like Mom," I said.

Tanner laughed. "You're right, Ryan." He lowered his voice. "Shut your face, Ace. Heh-heh-heh."

We floated along for a while. When we hit some quiet water, I blasted out with a song I'd made up:

"Going down the river with my brother, Tanner, In a stupid kayak that looks like a bananner."

"That's bad," Tanner said. "Even for you, that's bad."

I laughed. Tanner was Superstudent and Superhero, but I was Bad Song Champion. I made up the worst songs in the world. And my singing was even worse than my songs.

Hey, like my dad says, everybody's good at something.

"This is great," Tanner called out a few minutes later. "The Harrison boys riding on the Boulder River." He used his paddle to flick some water on me.

The cold water made me jump, and the kayak

rocked a little. "Just so we stay *on* the river and not *in* it," I said. "That water's freezing."

"Quit worrying," Tanner said. "The biggest danger you'll have today will be burning your tongue on a toasted marshmallow."

But he was wrong. Very wrong.

CHAPTER TWO

"Lift your paddle over your head," Tanner told me. "Arms straight."

I raised my paddle. "What's going on?"

"See where your hands are? That's where you want them when you paddle."

Tanner was right. As usual. It was easier to paddle that way.

"Okay," I said, "back there you said we were lucky. What did you mean?"

"We got a real break," Tanner said. "The river's a lot higher than it was last year. They must be letting extra water out of the dam. That's why you see all the leaves and wood floating around. And that log down there."

"Why is that a break?" I asked.

"Last year Brady and I had to carry the kayak a bunch of times. The water was too shallow. Besides, we should get a little white water now."

"White water? What do you mean?"

"You know. A few rapids. A little action."

"Oh, great," I said. "Maybe we'll get so lucky, we can flip over. Have ourselves a lucky swim."

Five minutes later, I thought we were going to get that lucky swim. We hit some rough water and bounced around. Then we scraped a boulder. The back of the kayak swung around, and we ended up floating downriver sideways. Right into some more rough water.

The kayak rocked and twisted. We hit a wave, and one side of the kayak rose up. I thought we were going over. "Ride 'em, cowboy!" Tanner yelled.

We bounced a few more times. Then Tanner got the kayak straightened out, and things were quiet again.

"Tanner," I called over my shoulder, "this is crazy. What are we doing on this wild river?"

Tanner laughed. "Two answers, Ryan. First, this is *not* a wild river. A wild river is a river that hasn't been dammed. And this one has a dam about five miles up the canyon."

"It's wild enough for me," I said. "I don't care what you call it."

"Second," Tanner went on, "what do you think we're doing here? We're having some fun. A little excitement. Instead of sitting around playing video games, we're out here doing something real."

I didn't bother to answer. You can't argue with Tanner.

We were in a deep canyon, steep on both sides. When I looked up, all I saw were trees and black cliffs. So I kept my eyes on the river, watching out for big rocks while I made up a new song.

When I was ready, I leaned back and blasted out:

"Paddling down the Boulder River,
Freezing water makes me shiver.
The place I'd rather be instead
Is back at home in my warm bed."

"That's bad," Tanner said. "But not as bad as most of your songs."

We were on smooth water, but the kayak started rocking. "What's going on?" I asked.

"We're fine. I'm going to be wiggling around for a while. Just keep us in the current."

The kayak started bouncing and tipping. "What are you doing back there? It feels like you're jumping up and down."

"I'm getting ready to fish," he said. "And I'm taking off this stupid life vest. It's in my way."

"Don't you need it?"

"Hey, Ryan, we're not going to flip. And even

if we did, the river's not that deep. I could stand up anywhere."

I tried to keep the kayak heading straight downstream. Sometimes that wasn't easy. It kept turning to the side.

"Pull off to your right," Tanner called. "I think there's a monster fish in that pool over there."

I shoved my paddle in the water and held it. The kayak turned that way. Then I paddled toward the shore, out of the current.

"Okay," Tanner said. "It's shallow now. Use your paddle to keep us right here."

I reached down with my paddle. It crunched on sand. The water was only a foot deep. Tanner let his line float downstream.

Right away his pole started bouncing. "Got one," he said. "I told you we'd have a fish dinner tonight." He reeled in his line. The fish was only about five inches long.

"Not a very big dinner," I said.

Tanner used a cloth to hold the fish. Then he

pulled out the hook with his special pliers. He held up the fish and laughed. "He wouldn't even be a mouthful." He dropped it back into the water.

"Will the fish be all right?" I asked.

"Sure," Tanner said. "That's why I use hooks with no barbs." He reached forward with his pole. "You try it, Ryan."

"That's okay," I said. "I'd probably hook the kayak and sink us."

"Try it!"

"You go ahead. I'm no good at that stuff. Too many things to do at once."

"Too many things at once? Come on, Ryan. You're the guy who does his homework, plays video games, and makes up songs—all at the same time." He flipped the line into the water, then shoved the pole into my hand. He used his paddle to keep the kayak in place. "Okay, now reel it in slow."

Right away I felt a pull. "Hey!" I yelled.

"Keep reeling," Tanner shouted. "And keep the tip of the rod high."

I kept reeling, but the fish pulled one way, then the other. "I think I got the monster!"

I brought the fish up close to the kayak. Tanner reached out with a net and lifted the fish out of the water. "Way to go," he said.

It was another five-incher. "Not exactly a monster," I said.

Tanner dropped the fish back into the water. "Hey, you did great." He nudged me. "And it was fun, right?"

"Right," I said.

"So let's see if his big brother is in there."

In the next ten minutes Tanner and I caught four more fish and let them go. They were all little. Maybe it was the same fish over and over.

I had time to make up a new song:

**"Play the banjo, beat the drum.
Tanner caught a fish the size of my thumb."**

Tanner surprised me by coming back with his own song:

**"This is my Boulder River song:
Ryan caught a monster one inch long."**

"Cut that out," I said. "I'm the singer, not you. Besides, my fish were bigger than yours."

"No way."

"Much bigger," I said. "At least half an inch."

Tanner picked up his paddle. "Let's keep moving. The real fishing is down at Grey Pine Creek. We'll camp where it flows into the river and walk upstream from there. You'll catch so many fish, you'll get tired of hauling them in."

"Maybe," I said.

"You'll see. Creek full of big trout, and almost nobody fishes it."

"Why not?"

"Too much work. It's a long way in there. Steep. And then you have to hike back out." He laughed. "Unless you're smart enough to kayak in. And nobody else does that."

"Why not?"

"Think about it, Ryan. All these boulders. You wouldn't dare do it in a regular kayak. Besides, the river's too shallow most of the time. We got lucky today."

We floated for a while. It was warm in the sunshine, and Tanner took off his shirt. He caught one more fish and let it go. "Bigger," he said. "But not big enough."

I looked downstream. Then I took a really good look. "Tanner," I said, "there's nothing but rocks up ahead."

He laughed and shouted, "Get ready for the chute!"

"The what?"

"The chute. River gets narrow for a minute. It's like a waterslide. No big deal. Just keep going straight."

I glanced over my shoulder. Tanner had put down his fishing pole and picked up his paddle.

I could hear the roar of water. That scared me a little. "It sounds like Niagara Falls," I yelled.

"Relax, bro. It's just a little waterslide."

Up ahead I could see a steep cliff on one side. On the other side were big black rocks. In the middle was a little opening. I hoped our kayak would fit.

"Keep 'er straight!" Tanner yelled.

The opening was wider than I'd thought at first. But I couldn't see anything past it. And the roar got louder and louder.

The nose of the kayak went straight into the opening. Then we were headed down too fast for me to do anything but hold on. We hit a pool at the bottom and shot ahead.

"All right!" Tanner yelled.

I glanced back. The chute didn't look very high. Or very steep. But I knew better.

"That was awesome," Tanner said. "Brady and I didn't get anything like that last year."

I waited a minute, then asked, "Tanner, didn't that scare you?"

"Sure," he said. "That's why it was fun."

"Maybe for you," I said. "I'm no hero."

He didn't answer. He was getting out his fishing

pole again. A few minutes later he hooked a fish, but it got away. I kept the kayak steady in the current.

"Hey, Ryan," he said, "that hero stuff—that's garbage. The only heroes these days are in video games or comic books."

"That's easy for you to say." I looked back at him for a second. "You ran into that burning house and saved that old guy."

"I just happened to be there. You'd have done the same thing. Later on, they made a big deal about it. But it was no biggie."

"I probably would have been too scared."

"You'd have been scared, sure. Everybody gets scared. But that wouldn't stop you. You do what you have to do."

"Maybe," I said. But I didn't believe it.

We drifted along for a while. It was warm in the sun. Until some icy water splashed on me. Which happened every minute or two.

"We're coming up on another chute," Tanner said. He reeled in his line, then picked up his paddle. "I think this one is shorter. Maybe a little steeper."

This time there was no cliff. Just big boulders on both sides of the river. I could hear the water roaring. The sound scared me. Maybe not as much as the first time, but I was still scared.

We did everything right. The kayak was straight, and we were in the middle of the river. I lifted my paddle and braced myself for the slide.

"Hang on, buddy!" Tanner yelled.

Just as we started down, I saw something ahead. A big black log. Right in the middle of the chute. With a jagged end pointing straight at us. And it wasn't moving. Not at all.

I opened my mouth to yell, but no words came out.

CHAPTER THREE

I watched the log get bigger and bigger. The kayak raced down the chute, heading straight for that jagged end. I dropped my paddle and tried to grab the slick, fat sides of the kayak. My fingers slid across the wet plastic.

At the last second the kayak veered away from the log. The idea flashed through my mind that a miracle was happening: we were going to miss the log.

Then I felt a hard jolt. Suddenly I was flying through the air. Somehow that didn't seem right. What was I doing in the air? Nothing made sense. It seemed like a dream.

But then I smacked the water headfirst and went under. That brought me out of the dream in a hurry.

The cold took my breath away. My nose and mouth filled with water. My eyes were open, but all I could see was bubbles. I started waving my arms and kicking. My head popped out of the water, and I sucked in air. Lots of air.

I looked around and realized that I was floating downstream. The life vest was holding me up. I kicked and paddled toward the shore. Then I shoved my feet down and stood up. The water was only waist deep.

I turned and looked back. Tanner was about ten feet behind me. He was floating with his arms out in front of him. But his face was in the water. And he wasn't moving.

I stood and looked at him for a second. I was

too shocked to do anything else. None of it seemed real.

Then I rushed toward Tanner. I had to do two things: get his face out of the water and drag him to shore. But I wasn't thinking straight. So I tried to do both at the same time. I grabbed his hair and lifted up his head; then I caught hold of an arm and tried to pull him along. I stumbled around, but I managed to move him into shallower water. It was slow going, and I had trouble keeping his head up.

Finally my brain started working again. The answer was so simple: I had to get him on his back.

I lifted his arm and hauled him across my knee. I grabbed his other shoulder and pulled as hard as I could. On the third try, I got him flipped over. Then I grabbed both of his arms and hauled him toward shore. I had to stop when the water was a few inches deep. Tanner's feet were dragging, and he was just too heavy.

I let go of his arms and knelt down by him. I held his head and got my first real look at his face.

What I saw scared me. His eyes were closed and his mouth was hanging open. He had a big purple spot on his forehead. Blood was oozing out of it.

I was afraid he was dead. He sure looked dead.

Right away I thought about doing mouth-to-mouth. Except I wasn't sure how to start. We'd been shown how to do it in Cub Scouts. But all the guys were joking around that night. Laughing about doing mouth-to-mouth with girls. I remembered the Scout leader getting mad at us, but that was about all I could remember.

Then Tanner coughed and started to throw up. Maybe that sounds disgusting. But right then it was beautiful. Tanner was alive. And breathing.

I held Tanner's head until he quit coughing. Then I used all my strength to drag him a little closer to shore, an inch or two at a time. I had to stop when we were in ankle-deep water. That was as far as I could go. The shoreline was all rocks. I couldn't lift Tanner. And even if I could have dragged him, those rocks would have torn him up. He didn't even have on a shirt.

I moved him around, one arm or one leg at a time. Soon he was flat on his back with his arms stretched out. Right then, I remembered one thing from the Cub Scouts lesson: I turned his face to the side, in case he got sick again.

I unfastened my life vest and threw it onto the shore. Then I pulled off my T-shirt and used it to wipe away the blood on his forehead.

It was terrible to look at that twisted face. Eyes shut. Mouth hanging open. It didn't look like Tanner's face at all. Just a bloody, scary mask.

His breathing was steady. But he was lying there in about three inches of that freezing water.

I had to do something. I couldn't leave him there. Maybe I could haul him across those rocks. Maybe. Even if it was hard on him.

I looked upstream for the first time. Our kayak was still stuck in the chute. Water was pouring over it. The log had gone through one side and was holding it there. The back of the kayak had flipped across the front. It looked kind of like a crooked hamburger bun.

Somewhere around there was our dry bag. I'd have to find it. I thought first about getting Tanner's sweatshirt. But then I realized that we had sleeping bags in there. That would be better. I could get one and put it under Tanner. I could slide him easier that way. And he wouldn't get so beaten up by the rocks.

I started upstream, looking for the dry bag. Tanner's life jacket was floating in the shallow water. I grabbed it and put it under his head. At least that got his head out of the water.

"Hang on, Tanner," I said. "I'll be right back." I hoped he could hear me, even though he wasn't conscious.

Below the chute was a deep pool. I waded toward it, staying out of the current. I kept looking into the pool, trying to spot that black dry bag. I hoped it had come flying out, the way I had.

My paddle was floating on the edge of the pool. I grabbed it and threw it to shore. The only other thing I saw was the coil of bear rope. It was sitting on the rocks at the bottom of the pool.

Moving closer, I could see what had happened. The log was right in the middle of the chute. One end was buried in the mud at the bottom of the pool. The other end was sticking through the kayak, holding it there, about a foot above the pool. Like a marshmallow on a fork. The back of the kayak was on top of the rest. The pumped-up side was bent in the middle to make two fat layers.

After looking everywhere else, I figured the dry bag was still in the kayak. It had been jammed so tightly into that front space that it must have stayed there. With the back end of the kayak flopped over the front, I couldn't see the bag. But I was sure it was there.

I looked back at Tanner, then dove into the water and swam straight toward the kayak. After a few strokes, I was in the main current. I dug in, kicking hard and moving my arms as fast as I could. For a minute I was moving upstream, getting closer to the kayak. But then I was just holding steady, swimming as hard as I could and not getting any closer.

I knew it was useless. The current was too strong. But I kept swimming for another minute. I hated to give up. But I finally turned sideways and let the current carry me toward shallow water.

I was mad. Wiped out by the river. I was sure it was going "Heh-heh-heh."

I glanced over at Tanner. He hadn't moved. I didn't know how long he could last in that water. Suddenly I remembered a video game I'd played. One of those stranded-on-a-desert-island games. In the game, if you stayed wet too long, your body temperature dropped. There was even a little thermometer on the screen. And if you didn't get warm quickly enough, you died.

I had to get that dry bag. I waded upstream as far as I could go. Then I held onto rocks and worked my way toward the chute. Soon the water was up to my chest.

Once I got to the edge of the chute, I was stuck. Water was roaring down. The spray was hitting my face. That kayak sandwich was still about three feet away and a foot above my head.

I climbed up the slippery rock as far as I could. My knees were still in the water. Then I made a leap for the kayak. I got my hand between the layers, but I couldn't hold on. My fingers slid over the plastic, and I was swept downstream.

I could almost hear the "Heh-heh-heh."

But this wasn't a video game. In those games, if you made a mistake and got killed, it was no big deal. You just started a new game.

I swam to the side. After checking on Tanner, I started upstream again. I didn't want to think about video games and being killed, but I couldn't help it. I'd never been in danger before. Video games were as close as I'd come.

Those games seemed silly right then. Battling aliens, fighting off pirates, crossing rivers full of alligators . . . But then I stopped walking and looked around. Maybe the games were silly, but I had learned one thing from playing them: if you tried something and it didn't work, you didn't keep doing it. You did something else.

I'd tried to grab the pumped-up part of the

kayak, and it was too fat. Nothing to hang on to. It didn't make sense to try again.

This time I'd go for the log. Maybe I could grab that and work my way up.

I climbed the rock again. My legs were shaking, but I stopped and checked the log. I figured out exactly where to jump and what to grab. Then I took in a big breath and sprang into the air. I hit the blast of water and reached out for the log. My fingers raked across it, then slid into the water. I tried to grab something with my other hand, but it was too late. I was already being swept downstream.

That was it. I was beaten.

I tried not to think about video games or anything else while I waded back to where Tanner was lying. He was still breathing all right, but his skin looked blue. Probably from the cold.

I was feeling the cold too. My arms were shaking, and my teeth were chattering.

It didn't make sense to go back upstream again. I couldn't get the dry bag. So I'd have to pull

Tanner out of the water without any help. There was nothing else to do.

I pulled. Again and again. I lifted and pulled. Raised his shoulder and pulled. Moved his leg to the side and pulled.

After all that, I had moved him about two inches.

I wanted to scream. I had to get him out of the water. But how?

CHAPTER FOUR

I was stuck. No matter how hard I tried, I wasn't strong enough to drag Tanner out of that freezing water. But I couldn't leave him there.

The only idea I'd had was to slide him along with the sleeping bag. But it was in the dry bag. Which was in the kayak. Which was hanging off the end of the log.

For a second I thought about making another leap at the kayak. But I knew better. I'd end up not being able to hang on. And I'd get swept downstream again.

It was the old video game business. There was no point in making the same mistake over and over. I had to try something else. Anything else.

And suddenly I thought of a new way. If I couldn't get at the kayak from the side, maybe I could do it from above. I could climb to the top of the chute. Then I could slide down and grab the kayak.

Maybe.

And maybe I'd go flying right by.

Then I remembered a video game I'd played a long time ago. In that game, my man had to find a rope to get down a cliff.

I had a rope. At the bottom of the pool. I could use that to lower myself.

I almost jumped into the water right away, but then I stopped myself. I had to move fast—but I had to move smart, too.

I ran along the edge of the water, then waded in. Back to the edge of the chute. The rope was about fifteen feet downstream. I took a long breath and dove. I swam hard until my hand touched bottom. Then the current carried me, and I grabbed the coil as I went by.

Once I had the rope in my hand, I felt better. I knew it wasn't a big deal—I was barely started. But I'd made a plan, followed it, and gotten what I needed. Everything seemed possible now.

I paddled out of the current, stood up, and hurried back upstream. "Hang on, Tanner," I shouted. "It won't be long now."

I kept looking at that kayak, stuck there in the chute with water roaring over it. The pumped-up side, bent over itself, looked like swollen yellow lips. I'd have to get between those lips to get the dry bag.

I could come down the rope and reach in from the side. But I'd be holding on to the rope with one hand. With all that water roaring over me.

Then I got a new idea: what if I popped those big balloon lips?

I almost smiled as I ran back toward Tanner. I had another plan.

All I needed was a knife.

I knelt down by Tanner and reached into one of his front pockets. "All right, Tanner. Where's your knife?" I dug into a pocket and pulled out a cloth and some little plastic boxes.

"Come on, Tanner. Where is it?" My fingers touched something metal. I grabbed it and pulled. It was his shiny pliers. I started to throw them onto the shore, then stopped. They were special fishing pliers. They had a knife blade built into one handle.

"I know you've got a better knife," I said. "But I just need to make one hole." I picked up the coil of rope and headed for the boulders.

Right away I needed my hands to climb. I stuck my head through the coil of rope—a fat necklace. The pliers were a bigger problem. I didn't have any pockets, and they were too heavy to carry in my teeth. So I jammed them into one of my soggy sneakers.

The climbing wasn't hard. But it took too long. Like everything else.

At the top of the chute, I looked around. I needed a tree to tie my rope to. The closest tree was on the other side of the river, so I'd have to go upstream and cross over. But then I looked at the boulder beside me. It was two feet across. Who needed a tree?

I uncoiled the rope and dragged one end around the boulder. I had learned some knots in Cub Scouts, but the only one I remembered was the granny knot. I did three of them, then yanked on the rope to be sure it would hold. And it did.

I grabbed the rope and stepped into the river. From there, the chute didn't look that steep. And the yellow kayak didn't look that far away.

Just in time I remembered the pliers. I had to get the knife ready now. Before I was in the chute.

I pried out the blade and tucked the pliers back into my shoe. The blade was sticking out, close to my ankle.

I hurried into the river. The water seemed even colder than before. Grabbing the rope with both hands, I dropped onto my stomach. The current carried me for a second. Then the rope went tight. I banged to a stop, with my arms stretched out. I used my legs to slide myself to the side of the chute. The current wasn't so strong there.

I worked my way down the rope, hanging on with one hand and reaching below for a new hold with the other. My stomach and knees scraped on rocks. That cold water swirled over me. I had to raise my head to get a breath.

I stopped just above the kayak. Then I grabbed the rope with both hands and kicked myself to the middle of the chute. The current pulled at me. And water poured over my head.

For a minute I hung there. Not moving. Holding tight with both hands.

Finally I let go with my upper hand and grabbed the rope just below the other hand. I lowered myself that way, inches at a time, until my shoes banged against the kayak. I got my feet steady and slowly squatted down. The water was pulling at me the whole time.

Under my feet was that big yellow balloon, just

waiting to be popped. I gripped the rope with one hand and dug the pliers out of my shoe with the other. I reached down with the knife blade and jabbed at the pumped-up section of the kayak. My knife slipped off to one side, and I almost dropped it.

I worked the knife into place again, then shoved hard. I moved my hand up and down, sawing at the spot. The plastic gave way, and the knife sank in.

I thought it would be like popping a balloon. But the air didn't come out that quickly. I worked the knife back and forth, making the hole bigger. Those yellow lips slowly flattened.

I dropped the pliers and grabbed the rope again. I lowered myself slowly and jammed my foot between the lips. The dry bag was still in there. I could feel it. Holding the rope with both hands, I used my leg to raise the upper section of the kayak. It was almost flat by then. Water came rushing in.

The dry bag popped free and floated downstream. I let go of the rope and swam after it.

It wasn't fair. I had worked so hard to get the bag free. And I had done it. But now the bag was being carried along by the current. It wasn't floating on top of the water. It was bouncing along on the bottom.

I dove down and made a grab for the bag but couldn't hold it. I swam with the current for a second, then reached down again. This time I didn't try to grab it. I just scooped it toward the shore.

Once the bag was out of the current, things were easier. I dragged the bag into shallow water, then picked it up.

"Hang on, Tanner," I yelled. "I'll have you out of there in no time."

I set the bag on the shore and undid the buckles. My hands were shaking, so everything was hard. And slow. Drive-you-crazy slow.

When I pulled out a sleeping bag, a rolled-up green thing came with it. I looked at it for a second before I figured out what it was: an old air mattress. I'd seen lots of plastic ones, but this was different. Green canvas, like a tent.

Right away I changed my plan. I didn't need a sleeping bag. Not when I had an air mattress.

I didn't see the pump. I thought maybe Tanner had left it in the van. But I didn't need it. My friend Kenny and I had used air mattresses before. They were just big balloons. You put your mouth on the stem and started blowing. Kenny and I had hot-air races to see who could fill his mattress first.

I flipped the cap off the stem and started in. Five breaths. Ten breaths. I got so dizzy that I had to stop for a minute and let my head clear. After about a hundred breaths, the air mattress was full enough. Finally. Five green tubes that looked like giant hot dogs.

I put the mattress in the water next to Tanner and went to work. It took me a long time to slide him onto that mattress. He was dead weight, and the mattress kept slipping away.

Once Tanner was on the mattress, I grabbed hold of the front and pulled. The mattress slid forward about three inches. I almost laughed. I could make it now. That slick mattress made the difference. It would be hard and slow, but I could make it.

It took forever. I pulled on the front. Then I moved to one side and scooted the mattress forward. Then to the other side. Then I pulled on the front again. And I kept shoving Tanner back to the middle of the mattress.

I didn't stop until Tanner's feet were out of the water. Then I unrolled a sleeping bag and covered him with it. His face was ghost white, but his breathing was steady.

"All right, Tanner," I said. "Soft bed. Nice and warm. You gotta love it."

And I loved it too. I had done it. The whole thing had seemed impossible, but I had done it.

By then I was exhausted. My knees were shaking, and my head seemed too heavy for my neck. I hauled out the other sleeping bag and spread it on the ground next to Tanner. I flopped down on it and didn't move.

I wasn't as comfortable as I expected. I could still feel the rocks underneath me. I'd seen another green air mattress in the dry bag, and I thought about getting it. But right then it was too much trouble.

The warm sun felt good on my back. I closed my eyes and let myself drift.

Before long, one of my stupid songs started bouncing around in my brain:

Kenny's lazy, William's worse,
But I'm the laziest guy in the universe.

Always before, that song had been a joke. But it wasn't funny now.

I tried not to listen. That song wasn't fair. I'd been working hard. Harder than I had in my whole life. And I'd gotten Tanner safely out of the water.

But the song wouldn't go away. I kept hearing it over and over. In some part of my brain, I knew the song was right: I *was* lazy. Tanner needed help, and I was loafing in the warm sun.

I rolled onto my side and looked at Tanner. I couldn't just lie there. I had to do something.

But what? That was the question. What could I do?

CHAPTER FIVE

anner hadn't moved. His forehead had stopped bleeding, and he had a little more color in his face. But he still looked bad.

I didn't know what to do. I knew boxers and football players got knocked out sometimes. But how did you get them to wake up?

I wondered if we'd studied this in Cub Scouts. If we had, I couldn't remember it now.

I moved over and put my mouth close to

Tanner's ear. "Tanner," I whispered. "Tanner?" His face didn't change.

Then I tried speaking louder. "Tanner. Can you hear me?"

Nothing.

"Tanner!" I yelled. "Tanner! Smiley! Tanner Harrison!"

No change.

I sat back and watched him. Here was my big brother. He looked terrible. I wanted to help him. More than anything in the world. But I couldn't think of anything to do.

If I'd been the one lying there, things would have been different. Tanner would have known what to do. But all I could do was sit there and look at him.

Now and then he snorted, and he groaned once. Whenever he made a sound, I yelled at him again.

It didn't help.

All we could do now was wait. Sooner or later we'd be rescued.

But it wouldn't be sooner. Dad wasn't supposed

to meet us until tomorrow. Two o'clock at some bridge.

I knew that when we didn't show up, he'd get somebody to look for us. But that was tomorrow. Late afternoon. If we were lucky. If Dad got worried soon enough. Otherwise, it would be dark, and they wouldn't be able to start looking until Monday.

So we were stuck. We might as well have been on a desert island.

Suddenly I realized how much this was like some of the desert island video games. First a shipwreck. Then getting everybody to shore. Then getting warm.

And finding food. In some of the games, you had to keep eating or your strength dropped.

At least the food part was easy for me. I went to the dry bag and got some peanut butter and crackers. I didn't realize how hungry I was until I took the first bite. Then I couldn't get enough.

Looking over at Tanner, I felt a little funny about stuffing myself with crackers. That didn't make any sense—starving myself wouldn't help him. But I felt funny anyway.

The crackers made me thirsty, so I dug into the dry bag and found the water bottle. I drank the whole bottle. Then I dug around and found the filter pump. At least I knew how to use that. I stepped into the river and pumped the bottle full of clean water.

I nibbled on crackers and tried to think. In the video games, after you got food and water and shelter, what did you do? Besides fight off dangerous animals and bad guys and pull somebody out of quicksand.

Easy. You set up signals for the rescue party.

That got me thinking about our rescue party. How would they find us? There was only one way: a helicopter. Nothing else would work.

I looked around. Twenty feet behind us were brush and trees. No helicopter could land here.

But across the river, things looked better. Downstream there was an open area. Rocky but flat. Big enough for a helicopter to land—I hoped.

But that would be tomorrow. Or maybe Monday.

I wondered if helicopters ever flew over this area. Maybe a pilot would spot us from the air. Still, even if somebody did fly over, what would they see? We'd just look like campers resting in the sun.

In one video game, you tramped big letters in the sand. A message big enough for airplane pilots to read.

I liked that idea. But it was impossible. What was I going to use to write a message?

I wished I had a can of spray paint. Bright green or bright red. I'd make letters six feet high. Big enough for any helicopter pilot to see.

It was silly to waste time wishing, and I knew it. I had no spray paint. No way to make a big bright sign.

But then I thought of that bright yellow kayak.

"What do you think, Tanner?" I said out loud. "Is that a dumb idea or what?"

Right then it seemed possible. I'd get the kayak free from that log. Then I'd haul it over to the far side. I'd cut it into pieces and use the pieces to write a message. A gigantic HELP.

A crazy idea, maybe. But it was better than sitting there looking at Tanner. And it just might work.

First I needed a knife. I had dropped the pliers when the dry bag came loose. But Tanner had another knife.

I lifted the sleeping bag and reached into his pocket. "Tanner," I shouted, "wake up! Somebody's stealing your stuff."

He didn't move.

Tanner's baggy shorts were cold and wet. I felt bad about that. I should have taken them off him right away.

Tanner groaned when I slid off his shorts. "Tanner," I shouted, "can you hear me?" But he just groaned once more.

Before I did anything else, I dug his jeans out of the dry bag. It wasn't easy getting them on him, but I thought they might help warm him. I got out his sweatshirt too and wrapped it around his shoulders.

I picked up the wet shorts and started digging. I found a knife in the third pocket. A regular old knife with two blades. Light enough to hold in my teeth. Right away I pried out the bigger blade.

I stood and looked at the kayak. Both sides were flat now, and it seemed to be bouncing a little. Maybe, with my help, it could float out of there.

I looked around for a stick and saw my paddle. Perfect. I picked up the paddle and stepped into the water. It seemed even colder than before.

Right then I realized what a dumb thing I'd done earlier. If I'd used my head, I could have made things much easier on myself. Instead of coming down the chute on a rope, I should have stayed down below and used the paddle to knock the dry bag loose. It would have saved me a lot of cold work.

I tried not to think about it. I'd done things the hard way. But at least Tanner was out of the water.

I stayed next to the rocks and waded out as far as I could. The spray from the chute spattered my face. I reached out with the paddle and jabbed at the kayak. It didn't move. Then I shoved the paddle underneath the kayak and tried to pry it loose. That didn't work either.

I shoved and jabbed for a long time, but the kayak stayed where it was. I started thinking about video games again. And about wasting time doing something that didn't work.

Finally I gave up and stepped back to rest. Standing there, I watched the bear rope bob up and down on the water.

Right away, I thought of another way to get the kayak loose. It meant getting soaked again. But I wasn't getting anywhere with the paddle.

First I went back to shore and put on my life vest. Then I waded out and used the paddle to bring the rope over. Keeping hold of the rope, I threw the paddle toward shore. "Here goes nothing," I mumbled, and put the knife handle in my mouth.

I held on to the rope and waded into the water. When I was chest deep, the life vest lifted me off the rocks. I squeezed the rope and kicked toward the log. Water beat down on my head and shoulders. I got one leg over the log, then worked my way higher. I kept scooting up until my head bumped the kayak.

I wrapped my legs around the log and held tight to the rope with one hand. With the other, I took the knife and started slicing. First I cut around the spot where the log had gone through. I made the hole bigger and bigger. Then I sliced up the side.

It was slow work. The icy water was pulling at me, and I couldn't see what I was doing. But I kept reaching out and slicing. And slicing some more.

Then, all at once, the kayak gave way and smashed into me. I flopped backward and went underwater. The kayak was on top of me, holding me down.

It was like something out of a nightmare. I tried to dive down to get free, but the life vest held me up. I pushed and yanked at the plastic on top of me. My lungs ached for air, but I was trapped.

A thought flashed through my mind: *This is the goofiest thing I've ever done. I'm going to be drowned by a flat kayak.*

Then my brain started working again. I'd been flopping around like a fish out of water. I knew better than that.

I reached up with both hands and shoved the kayak to one side. Then I shoved it again. On the third shove, my head finally popped above the water. I sucked in tons of air.

My foot banged against rocks. I put both feet down and stood up. I was waist deep in the water. The kayak was off to my right, hardly moving.

I stood for a minute and caught my breath. Now that I was safe, the whole thing was almost funny. Almost.

I dragged the kayak toward the far shore. It was heavy—flat now but partly full of water. Once I hauled it onto dry land, most of the water drained out.

I was ready to cut the kayak into strips to make

my HELP sign. Except for one thing: the knife was gone.

I turned and looked at the pool below the chute. Somewhere in there was the knife. The pliers too.

I flopped down on the rocks. I was too tired to do anything else.

After a few minutes, I jumped up. Then I caught myself. This was like playing video games. When I got in a hurry, I made mistakes. And I didn't need any more of those. So I stood there on the bank until I had a plan.

First I checked to be sure the rope was still there. It was bobbing on top of the water, just like before. I went downstream and crossed where the water was shallower. Moving upstream, I stopped to check on Tanner. No change.

Then I went on and got my paddle again. I took off my life vest, waded in, and used the paddle to snag the rope. I kept trying to see into the pool. All I could see was bubbles, caused by the crashing water. But the knife had to be there somewhere.

After a minute I spotted something shiny about ten feet downstream. Those silver pliers.

I held on to the rope and slid into the water. The rope kept me from being swept downstream while I kicked out to the middle of the pool. When I was about five feet upstream from the shiny pliers, I made a quick dive and grabbed them.

For once, everything worked the way it was supposed to.

For the kayak, I had another simple plan. I'd cut strips to spell out HELP. I wrote the word in the sand and saw that I'd need thirteen strips—five long and eight shorter.

It wasn't a bad plan. It just didn't work. The plastic was too hard to cut. And I couldn't cut in a straight line.

Besides that, I didn't have enough plastic. Even if I could cut the kayak into thirteen strips, they would be too small. Nobody could see them from the sky.

All that work for nothing.

It would have been neat. A big yellow HELP sign.

I plopped down on the rocks and looked at the kayak. I found myself thinking about video games again. If something didn't work—

I sat up straight. I couldn't make a HELP sign. But maybe I could do something else. Maybe a big yellow X.

I grabbed the pliers and went to work. It took me a long time, but I managed to cut the kayak into two pieces. I dragged those pieces to the middle of the open area and made my X. A little crooked. But an X all the same.

If somebody flew over, maybe they'd see that yellow X. Maybe they'd wonder what it was and fly lower. Then maybe we could wave them down.

It wasn't a giant HELP sign. But it was the best I could do.

— — —

When I got back, Tanner looked the same. His breathing was loud but steady. I knelt down by him and shouted his name. He didn't move.

I sat in the sun and ate some more crackers and peanut butter. I kept looking up at the sky. No planes. No helicopters. Not even a cloud.

I wondered what time it was. Then I remembered that Tanner had a watch. He wasn't wearing it, so it had to be in one of his pockets.

I picked up the wet shorts and started digging. "Tanner, wake up," I shouted. "You're being robbed again."

I found the watch in a side pocket. It said twelve-thirty.

That couldn't be right. It had to be later than that. I figured the watch was broken. But I watched the seconds tick off.

So it was only twelve-thirty. In twenty-eight or thirty hours, somebody might start looking for us. If we were lucky. And so far our luck had been rotten.

I glanced over at Tanner's white face. He needed help soon. Not thirty hours from now. I had to do something. Something besides sitting there wishing for a helicopter to rescue us.

CHAPTER SIX

"**H**ey, Tanner," I shouted, "wake up and I'll sing you an awesome song."

He didn't move.

"Okay, wake up and I promise *not* to sing. For a whole day. For a week. For a month!"

I hated just sitting there. I wanted to do something, but I couldn't think of anything. Except to hang around and watch my brother.

I wondered if I was watching him die. I tried not

to think that way, but I couldn't help it. He'd been out cold for a long time. That was bad. Really bad. I didn't need first-aid training to know that.

No matter how I tried, I couldn't get rid of the terrible thoughts. Along with other horrible things, I started thinking about the night ahead. Somehow that scared me most of all.

I had the feeling that Tanner would die that night. I'd be sitting around, doing nothing, and Tanner would die.

"No!" I shouted, and stood up. I had to go for help now.

I was at the bottom of a steep canyon. I couldn't go up the river. And I couldn't go down. So I'd have to climb out.

I looked across the river, past the open area where I'd put the yellow X. I could see brush and trees and big rocky cliffs. I had to tilt my head back just to see where the cliffs met the sky.

But somewhere up there was a road. This morning we had been on that road. We'd looked down from there and seen the river. If I could get up to that road, I could get help.

I kept looking up at those cliffs. Wondering if I could find a way up. I had to try. It was the only chance I had.

I worried about Tanner waking up while I was gone. I wished I had a pencil and paper so I could leave him a note. Just in case.

If he did wake up, he'd be thirsty. Maybe even hungry. I pumped the bottle full of clean water again and set it beside his head. I put the box of crackers next to it. And his watch. Maybe he'd wake up and wonder how long he'd been out. I hoped so.

At the last minute I dragged the whole dry bag over next to him. That way he could reach anything he wanted. And I fixed it so that it kept the sun off his face.

When everything was ready, I stood there and looked down at Tanner. "Hang on, Tanner," I told him. Then my throat got really tight. "You better not die on me."

I grabbed the sweatshirt and jeans Tanner had packed for me. I carried them across the river, then put them on. The dry jeans felt good on my cold legs.

I passed my X and started looking for a trail. Ahead of me were thickets of willows. Above them, the hillside was covered with bushes and trees. It looked like a jungle.

I kept having horrible thoughts. Like telling Mom that Tanner was dead. And wondering where he'd be buried. Those thoughts were like nightmares. Worse, because I was awake.

Trying to get those things out of my mind, I started talking to myself, even singing:

**"I'm going up. I will not stop
Until I reach the mountaintop."**

I found a break in the willows and headed uphill. Soon I was in brush higher than my head. I tried to hurry, but it was slow going. I zigzagged, looking for openings, and ended up crawling most of the time.

Somewhere along the way, I started thinking of the climb as a game. I was headed up the mountain, taking on the Mountain Demon. To keep away the bad thoughts, I kept singing about what I was doing:

"Crawl on my belly to an open space,
Spiderwebs all over my face.
Crawl under bushes, around that tree,
Mountain Demon can't stop me."

I was breathing too hard to really sing. But I kept it up, even when I had to whisper.

The game and the singing worked for a while. But pretty soon I'd catch myself thinking about Tanner in the dark. And I'd break out singing again. Louder. Trying to chase away the nightmare thoughts.

After a long time, I came to an open area. No

bushes, no trees. Just a gigantic pile of rocks. I was happy until I looked up—and saw where the rocks had come from.

Above me were rocky cliffs. The same dark color as the rocks I was standing on.

I could almost hear the Mountain Demon laugh.

I tried to find a way around the cliffs. I stayed on the piles of rock and moved sideways for a while.

Nothing. Just more cliffs.

I stopped and looked up again. The cliffs weren't straight up and down. There were cracks and humps and ledges.

Maybe I could work my way up. Maybe.

I had two choices. Either I went up the cliffs, or I gave up and went back down the hill. To sit by Tanner and wait for dark.

So really there was only one choice.

I scooted across the rocks until I found a good place to climb. Where I started, the going was steep but not straight up and down. Above that was a split in the cliffs, a crack that seemed to go all the way to the top.

I felt better. I had found a way out.

For a few minutes I had forgotten about the game. But I began to sing again when I started climbing:

"Mountain Demon, I'm not through. This is level number two."

I liked that idea. Same game. Different location. And I was still moving up.

I had climbed a few walls at the YMCA gym. (Tanner thought I'd enjoy it. Even when I told him I didn't.) I knew how you were supposed to do it: you hold on with three—two feet and one hand or two hands and one foot—and reach with the fourth. But that's easier on the gym wall. There are lots of handholds. And you're wearing a safety harness.

I moved up quickly. I kept my eyes steady. No looking down.

For a while I counted. Then I started singing to myself as I climbed:

"Hand is one. Foot is two.
Three is hand, and four is shoe."

The same dumb song over and over. I was too busy to come up with anything else.

In no time I was at the bottom of the crack. The crack was bigger than I expected. And it was rough enough along one edge to give me good handholds.

I moved up at a slow, steady pace, singing that same song. I tried to keep my mind fixed on each move. But I still thought about Tanner now and then.

The crack started getting smaller. And my song got much slower.

Then I looked up but couldn't see anything to grab. I glanced to the left. Then to the right. Finally I held on with both hands and leaned back for a better look.

Nothing above me but slick, solid rock. Straight up and down for at least ten feet.

I couldn't go any farther. Dead end. The Mountain Demon had struck again.

I had to go back down.

Just thinking about it scared me. It had been hard enough going up, when I'd been able to look at each handhold before I grabbed it. Now I wouldn't be able to see where I was going. And I was way up high.

I could almost feel myself falling. I held tight to the rock with both hands, listening to my heart beating loud.

I stayed like that for a minute or two. My stomach hurt, and I kept tasting peanut butter.

Then I thought about Tanner lying by the river. I had to settle down. He was depending on me. Even if he didn't know it.

I took a slow, deep breath, then reached down with my left hand. Once I had a good grip on a rock, I reached down with my right foot until it hit something solid. Then I held on tight with both hands and slowly shifted my weight onto that foot.

That was the way it went. No more singing. No more game. Just one careful move. Then another. Then another. Always with two hands gripping hard before I reached down with my foot.

Finally the crack got wider and wider. I knew I was getting close to the bottom. I wanted to hurry. But I stayed with the same steady movements. And I didn't look down.

Then both feet were on solid rock at the bottom of the crack. I closed my eyes and leaned against the rock. I had made it.

After resting for a minute, I started looking for another way to go up. I was still about forty feet up from the rock pile at the bottom. I hated the idea of climbing down there and starting over.

I was looking off to the side, and stepped that way. Whatever I stepped on crumbled under my foot. I stumbled in that direction and lost my handhold. I reached back, but my hand touched nothing but air. My stomach smacked the rock, and I went sliding down.

I tried to grab on to something. Anything. But I

kept sliding. And sliding. Down, down. My chin banged on something, and my head bounced back. And I kept sliding and sliding. All the way down to the rock pile at the bottom.

When my feet hit something solid, I crumpled into a ball. Little rocks, sliding with me, bounced off my back.

I was lucky. Instead of sliding, I could have tumbled backward and taken a fall. But right then I didn't feel lucky at all. I just lay there on the rocks. I didn't know how bad I was hurt. My whole body was shaking.

After a minute or two, my breathing slowed down. I started by moving my fingers. Then my hands. Then my feet. Everything still worked.

I was scratched-up and sore. My chin stung like crazy, and blood was dripping down onto my sweatshirt. But I was still in one piece.

I was through climbing. Maybe somebody, like Tanner, could have climbed out of there. But I couldn't. I didn't even look at the cliffs again. The game was over.

I turned around and started back toward the river. I tried not to think about anything. But I was sure the Mountain Demon was laughing his head off.

I couldn't even go back the way I'd come. I lost the trail right away. So I crawled through brush again. And fought my way through the willows.

By the time I got to the river, sweat was pouring off me. I thought about diving into the water, clothes and all. But I caught myself just in time. My jeans and sweatshirt were dirty and bloody, but they were dry. Later, when it got cold, I'd need dry, warm clothes. I pulled them off, then waded in.

The water was too cold to feel good. Especially when it hit all my scratches and scrapes. My whole body was stinging and burning. Instead of swimming, I washed off quickly and waded across the river.

"Tanner," I shouted, "wake up! I'm back."

He didn't move.

I flopped down beside him. "I'm sorry, Tanner. I

tried. I did the only thing I could think of. But I couldn't make it. And I just about got killed."

Tanner groaned quietly. He almost seemed to be answering me. But his eyes were still closed, and his face had that same empty look.

I drank the water I'd left for him. "Now what?" I said.

What else could I do but sit there and watch Tanner die?

CHAPTER SEVEN

I reached over and checked Tanner's watch. Almost one-thirty. I was amazed. I was beat up and beat out. But the whole trip up the mountain had taken less than an hour.

And now we were stuck. There was nothing to do but wait. And wait. And wait.

All of a sudden I was mad. Plain old ticked-off mad. "Tanner," I yelled, "this is all your fault! Every bit of it! I didn't want to come on this stupid trip. And you knew it. But you always have to get your way."

Tanner just lay there with his mouth hanging open. It was like yelling at a rock.

I used the pump to filter some more water. Then I sat down and munched on crackers. I kept my eyes on the river. I didn't want to look at those cliffs.

Tanner had said that guys hiked in to fish on Grey Pine Creek. But the land had to be different down there. I couldn't believe anybody could hike in to where we were.

I looked across the river at my yellow X. I wished I hadn't cut up the kayak. I should have tried to get it off that log and patch it. Then maybe I could have gone down the river to the mouth of that creek.

I might have found fishermen there. Guys who could go for help.

Even if nobody was there, I could take their trail and hike out myself.

But the kayak was cut in two. Like Humpty Dumpty, it couldn't be put back together again.

Tanner moaned and shifted one leg. "Tanner!" I shouted. "Tanner! Can you hear me?"

His face had the same dead-man look. But at least he'd moved. That seemed like a good sign.

I looked up at the empty sky. No helicopters. No miracles in sight.

Then I looked back at Tanner, stretched out on that green mattress. Seeing him like that reminded me of something. Last summer my friend Kenny and I had blown up air mattresses and used them in his swimming pool. Most of the time we just lay on them and soaked up the sun. But sometimes we played battleship and tried to knock each other into the water.

I ran over to the dry bag. Who needed a kayak? I had an air-mattress battleship.

I unrolled the other mattress and started blowing. Five breaths, then rest a second. Then five more.

Everything seemed possible now. I'd head down the river and get help at Grey Pine Creek.

I felt good about the new plan. But I also felt a little stupid. I should have thought of this plan first. That way I could have skipped that whole rotten climb. And that slide down the mountain that had scraped off half my skin.

And I wouldn't have wasted all that time. If I'd been smarter, I might have been at Grey Pine Creek already.

Once the mattress was full, I put water and crackers next to Tanner's head and put the dry bag back in place.

"Hang in there, Tanner," I said. "This time I won't be back without help." As soon as I said that, I started to get scared. If I went down the river, Tanner was stuck here by himself. What if he woke up and needed my help?

But Tanner needed a doctor now. Today. Not tomorrow or Monday. I still had the feeling that he wouldn't make it through the night unless I got help.

I grabbed the mattress. I was going down the

river. It might be another mistake. I'd made plenty of them already. But I had to try. I wasn't going to sit there and watch him die.

I decided to wear my sweatshirt and jeans. They were filthy and bloody, but I thought they might protect my arms and legs. Mainly, though, the jeans had pockets, so I could carry the pliers. I probably didn't need them, but I liked having them. Mostly for the knife.

I shoved two granola bars into other pockets. Their foil wrappers would keep them dry.

Finally, I strapped on the life vest. It was still wet. And cold.

I checked Tanner once more. His face was shaded, and he could reach everything. "Okay, Tanner," I said. "Take it easy." My throat was so tight I could hardly talk.

At the last minute I grabbed his watch and slipped it on my wrist. I wanted to keep track of the time.

I pushed the mattress into the water, then flopped onto it. All my scrapes and scratches stung when the water hit them. Lying on my stomach, I used my hands to paddle into the current, then grabbed the sides of the mattress. I was on my way.

The mattress held me up, but water sloshed over it. My chest and stomach were never dry. Somehow it was colder to have only part of me wet. Soon my teeth were chattering.

As I headed downriver, I started thinking about Tanner. Wondering if I should have left him. It was too late to change my mind, but I kept thinking about him up there alone. What if some animal—like a bear—came along?

I didn't need nightmare thoughts like that. I had trouble enough. My mattress was a rotten boat. It kept trying to turn sideways. And it kept drifting out of the current. A few times I got spun around and ended up floating down backwards.

To keep from thinking, I started singing again. That got me remembering my last game. Being wiped out by the Mountain Demon.

But I wasn't going to get wiped out this time. I

was handling the mattress a little better, and I was moving along pretty well. I figured I could beat the River Demon:

> **"Moving fast and floating free.**
> **River Demon can't stop me."**

I didn't sing loud, but I kept making noise. Sometimes it was the same verse over and over. Once in a while, I made up a new one:

> **"Watch that boulder on the right.**
> **I have just begun to fight."**

Sometimes I had to use my hands to paddle. And I had to be careful not to move quickly. If I did, I'd get off balance and end up sliding into the water.

I checked the watch every few minutes. And I kept looking ahead for Grey Pine Creek. It couldn't be that far. That's what I kept telling myself, anyway.

Floating along, I heard something. I stopped singing and listened. That sickening roar. No way to mistake it. I jammed down my hand to turn the mattress and paddled into shallow water.

When I stood up, the roaring was louder. And I could see the place where the river narrowed. Another chute.

I was taking no chances. No more chutes for me. I hurried to shore, dragging the mattress behind me.

Right away I had to decide. I was going around the chute. No question about that. But should I let the air out of the mattress?

It was already two-fifteen. I hated to take the time—and the energy—to blow up the mattress again.

I tried carrying it. But that wasn't easy. For a while I held it against my side with one hand. Then I bent forward and walked with it on my back, using both hands to hold it in place. That worked until I needed a hand for climbing.

I finally gave in and let out the air and rolled it

up. That way I could carry it under one arm and use both hands if I needed to. And I did need to in a few spots.

I climbed over boulders, then down through brush. I didn't get a good look at the chute until I was below it. It was a little steep but not very long. I figured I could have handled the trip down. And I would have saved fifteen minutes.

But I had made it past a bad spot. I felt good about that. The River Demon wasn't going to stop me.

I blew up the mattress again and waded back into the river. My clothes had dried a little by then. So the water froze me all over again. Right away I started to sing:

"Water's freezing. So am I.
Wish I had some cherry pie."

A stupid song. Especially when I sang it over and over. But it kept me from thinking—most of the time.

I was learning to handle the mattress. Slow movements. Short strokes. I stayed in the current and floated along.

After a while I relaxed a little. Laid my head sideways on the mattress to rest my neck. I even quit singing. I started thinking about the campground up ahead. And the guys who would go for help.

By the time I heard the roar, it was too late. I shoved a cupped hand into the water, and the mattress turned sideways. I felt it sliding across my stomach. I tried to grab on, but I was off balance by then. The far side of the mattress rose into the air, and I was dumped into the water.

I must have been yelling, because my mouth was wide open when I went under. Water filled my mouth and nose, choking me. In just a second, the life vest popped me up to the surface, coughing and spitting.

I was moving fast by then, swept along by the current. I reached down with my feet but couldn't touch bottom.

I looked ahead and saw the mattress disappear into the chute. I was about a second behind it.

I leaned back and got my feet in front of me. If I banged into a rock, I wanted to do it with my shoes. Not my head.

Then I was in the chute. It was all noise and splashing water. I was thrown one way, then the other. My shoulder bounced off a rock. All I could do was clench my teeth and wait for it to be over.

The first thing I noticed was the quiet. Suddenly the roar was behind me. I looked up and saw the mattress off to the side. I swam over to it and hauled it into knee-deep water. Then I flopped down onto it and eased into the current.

I didn't look back at the chute. I had no idea how long it was or how steep. And I didn't want to know.

I'd been lucky. But I wasn't going to try my luck again. After that, I kept listening for any change of sound. And I kept my eyes fixed on the river in front of me.

Ten minutes later, I spotted something green up

ahead. Not a natural green, though. It was the green you see on tents.

I smiled for the first time. This time I had won the game, beaten the River Demon. I'd made it to the campground.

I just hoped there was a good strong camper there. Somebody who could go for help in a hurry.

I paddled into shallow water, then slid off the mattress. I dragged it onto the shore, then ran for the campground.

I thought about yelling, but I didn't see anybody. I saved my breath and headed straight for that green tent.

Going closer, I saw how small the campground was. Just a flat, open spot with two or three fire pits. I didn't slow down, but I kept looking in all directions.

And saw nothing. The place was empty except for that green tent back in the trees.

About twenty feet away from it, I stopped and stared. The green tent wasn't a tent at all. It was just an old tarp. Somebody had draped it over logs to make a shelter, the sort of thing you'd get under in a rainstorm. It looked like it had been there for months. Maybe years.

Nobody there. Nobody at all.

I could almost hear the River Demon laughing.

CHAPTER EIGHT

I looked around the empty campground and yelled. No words. Just noise. I couldn't hold it in anymore. I yelled and yelled.

It didn't help much. I was still mad. At everything and everybody. Mostly at myself.

I'd left Tanner alone so that I could come here. All the way down the river, I'd been picturing some supercamper. He'd go racing up the mountain for help while I lay in the sun.

I'd been playing my game, fighting the river all the way. And I'd made it. I thought I'd won. But there was nobody here. No supercamper. Nobody at all.

I should have known better.

I staggered over to a log and flopped down on it. The sun was warm on my face, but my wet jeans kept me shivering. I thought about taking them off but didn't. Too much trouble.

I sat there for a few minutes. I thought about getting out a granola bar but didn't.

Finally I pulled myself to my feet. It was time to get real. No supercampers here. The only person who could climb out of there was me. Tanner's little brother. Tanner's freezing, exhausted, mad little brother.

I headed past the fire pits, looking for the trail. My wet sneakers squished and squirted with each step.

I spotted one trail and started to follow it. But it split into two trails, and I could see another a few yards away.

I stopped and tried to think. Just below me was Grey Pine Creek. I could see where it flowed into the river. But the road we'd come in on that morning was on the other side of the river.

Was the trail over there? Or was the trail on this side, leading up to a different road?

Tanner had probably told me, when he was talking about guys hiking in to fish. But I hadn't really listened. I had figured Tanner would take care of everything.

I moved into an open area and looked across the river at black cliffs. They seemed even higher than the ones upstream. I decided the trail had to be on this side.

I picked out the biggest trail and hurried along it. Other trails split off every fifty steps or so, but they all led down to the creek.

My trail got smaller and smaller. I was afraid it was just a trail for fishermen. I looked at my watch and decided to give it five more minutes.

A little farther on, the trail split. One fork headed uphill. I stopped and studied it. It zigzagged back and forth, moving higher, until it disappeared into the trees. It seemed to be heading in the right direction. But it seemed too small to be the trail out of there.

I hated to start climbing unless I was sure.

I stood at the fork and tried to decide. Somewhere around there was a trail that led to a road. Maybe this was it. If I was lucky, maybe I could follow it and get help.

But, so far, my luck had been terrible. Why would it change now? I might follow that trail for hours and get nowhere. I pictured myself walking on and on while the sun was going down.

I couldn't take a chance. There was only one sure way out: down the river. It might take a long time, but sooner or later I'd get to a bridge.

A bridge. Somewhere downstream. A mile? Ten miles? I had no idea. Just somewhere downstream. I hadn't bothered to listen to Tanner, so that was all I knew.

But what else did I need to know?

I looked at my watch: three-thirty. Almost half an hour since I'd left the river. Too much time wasted already.

I turned and ran back toward the campground.

It probably sounds funny, but right then I felt better than I had since I left Tanner. Everything was decided now. I was going down the river. I didn't know how long it would take, but it didn't matter. There was no other choice.

Before I went into the water, I added some air to the mattress. It wasn't easy, because I was already out of breath. The mattress took lots of air. I wondered if it had sprung a leak. But I didn't worry about it for long. Leak or not, I was headed downstream.

The running had warmed me, so the first steps into the cold river were hard. I ended up yelling again. It didn't help much.

I carried the mattress into knee-deep water, then flopped down on it. I paddled for a minute, then let the current take me away.

Next stop: the bridge. All I had to do was hang on and wait.

— — —

After Grey Pine Creek, the river seemed a little wider and a little deeper. The current was strong. I kept the mattress steady and watched out for rocks.

I hummed a little, but I didn't feel like singing. I looked at my watch every two or three minutes. It was like one of the video games where you have to finish all the jobs before the time runs out. You have to hurry, but you try not to think about time. But you can't help it.

I could almost hear the clock ticking away: Three-fifty. Three-fifty-two. What if I couldn't make it to the bridge before dark? What if it was so dark that I couldn't see the bridge? I might go right past it. The River Demon would love that.

That kind of worrying was dumb, and I knew it.

All I could do was stay in the current and keep moving. There was no way to speed up. Still, I couldn't help thinking about floating along in the dark.

I heard noise up ahead. I looked up, expecting some kind of chute. But I could see the river far in front of me.

Closer, though, were boulders and rough water. I could see little waves rising in front of me. I paddled to the right to stay clear of a big black rock.

The waves rocked my mattress enough to make me grab on with both hands. I bounced through the water for a minute, spun sideways, then bounced a little more. A little action from the River Demon. But it couldn't dump me off my boat.

If things had been different, it might have been fun. But right then nothing was fun.

After that, the river got wider and shallow. Not even a foot deep. And the current slowed. I had to look at the shore to be sure I was still moving. I felt like yelling again.

I was almost sorry I'd brought Tanner's watch. In some ways, it made things worse. I ground my teeth when it showed four o'clock.

I took a deep breath and looked ahead. No bridge. But there was something black on the shore. At first, I thought it was a boulder. But then I realized that the black thing was moving.

A bear. That was all I needed. A bear.

The River Demon was *not playing fair.*

CHAPTER NINE

The bear was on my right. So I shoved my left
hand into the water. The mattress turned that
way, and I eased out of the current. I caught hold
of a boulder and held the mattress in place. I lay
there, without moving, and watched.

The bear was about fifty yards downstream from
me. It was on the shore, a few feet from the river.
It seemed to be eating something.

I didn't know what to do. I thought about

paddling over to the bank and waiting for it to leave. At least there would be the river between us.

Maybe I'd be safer onshore. I could run if the bear started across the river.

The bear kept its nose to the ground. What was it eating? What did bears eat, anyway?

I didn't know much about bears. I'd read a book about them a long time back. Maybe third grade. I sort of remembered that they had bad eyesight but great noses. And they were fast runners. Much faster than you'd think.

That didn't make me feel any better.

That spring, mountain lions had been seen close to our town. So we'd been told over and over how to scare them away: you were supposed to yell and hold your arms high to make yourself look bigger. I wondered if that would work with a bear.

I held on to the boulder and watched the bear eat. And took quick glances at my watch. Four-oh-five. Four-oh-eight. Four-ten.

The bear raised its head and walked a few

steps. "Keep going," I whispered. "Keep going." But then it lowered its head and started eating again. It seemed to be in no hurry at all.

But I was. Four-fifteen came and went. I kept thinking about Tanner. And wondering what time the sun went down.

At four-twenty, I couldn't stand to wait any longer. The bear had its back to the river. And it was busy eating. I had to try slipping past.

I let go of the rock and eased the mattress back into the current.

The mattress started moving downstream. I couldn't change my mind now. All I could do was keep floating. And watching the bear. It seemed to get bigger and bigger.

The bear raised its head again and started walking. Moving in the same direction I was. It had a kind of rolling walk. Its head swung back and forth with each step.

The current was moving faster than the bear. So I was getting closer and closer. I used one hand to steer the mattress toward the other shore. I wanted to be as far away as possible. But I had to stay in the current.

Then I was even with the bear. Close enough to see leaves and bits of brown grass stuck in its fur.

For a minute, I forgot about everything but that fantastic animal. I was scared, I guess. But mostly I was amazed. A bear right there, moving along with me.

The bear stopped and raised its head high. Maybe it was wondering what that weird thing in the river was. I probably didn't look good to eat. The bear kept smelling the air and turning its head from side to side.

I wonder what kind of smell the bear got from me and my dirty, wet clothes and the mattress. What did it think I was?

Finally the bear lowered its head and walked away from the water.

By that time, I was looking back over my shoulder. I glanced ahead for a second to check for rocks. When I looked back again, the bear was gone.

I was still excited. My first thought was *Wait till I tell Tanner*. But that brought everything back. I bit down hard and tried to keep my teeth from chattering.

I started to sing again to keep from thinking. I was too tired and cold to make anything up, so I sang a song from last summer. I'd used it to tease my mother:

> **"What a bummer!**
> **Mom thinks I get dumber**
> **During the summer.**
> **Wants me to read, wants me to write.**
> **Wants me to study French at night.**
> **'Paint some pictures, build some frames.**
> **And do not play those video games!'"**

Last summer. I wanted to be back there. Back when my biggest problem was Mom fussing at me for wasting time.

So I sang that song. Over and over. Trying to keep my mind on last year. Trying not to think about Tanner. Or the hour I'd wasted on the mountain. Or the time I'd wasted at Grey Pine Creek.

I went through a few stretches of choppy water without any problems. Every minute or two I looked ahead, hoping. No bridge.

I never stopped singing. After a while my song got quieter. In fact, sometimes I don't think I said the words out loud. But I kept singing.

And I kept floating downstream. Too slow, of course. But I was staying in the current and doing all I could.

Then, on a stretch of easy water, my hands started shaking worse than usual. And my legs did the same.

I had to stop.

I hated the idea. Time was running out. It was already four-forty-five. I only had a few hours of daylight left. But I had to get warm.

I spotted a flat area up ahead. Except for some shadows along the edge, it was still in the sun. I steered my mattress into shallow water and slid off. I fell twice trying to get to shore. My legs just didn't work right.

Out of the water, I worked and worked to get my life vest unbuckled. Then I dragged myself across rocks to a stretch of sand. I wanted to flop down on that sand and never move again.

I sat down hard but didn't lie down. Instead, I began pulling up my soaking sweatshirt. Once the sweatshirt was off, I kicked off my shoes and started squirming out of my soggy jeans.

It took forever to pull off those jeans. When I was finally free, I threw them aside and collapsed on the sand. I still had on a wet swimsuit, but I didn't care.

I lay on the warm sand for a long time. With the sun on my back, I soon quit shivering. My body felt heavier and heavier. I could feel myself drifting off to sleep.

"No!" I shouted. I dragged myself to my knees and looked at the watch. Five-oh-five. I grabbed my sweatshirt. It was still sopping wet. I wrung out some of the water. But I couldn't stand to put it on.

I ended up tying the sweatshirt around my waist. I gritted my teeth when the wet sleeves touched my bare stomach. My jeans were right by my foot. "No way," I said out loud. I pulled on my wet tennis shoes and shivered when my feet hit the cold. I stood up and hurried back toward the river.

I strapped on my life vest again and dragged the mattress into the water. I felt funny about leaving my jeans behind. That probably sounds silly. But it felt strange to go off and leave my good jeans.

Before I shoved off, I remembered the granola bars and pliers. Back there in my jeans pockets. But I didn't even look that way. I was running out of time.

I was already shivering when I flopped down on

the mattress. I decided right then that I wouldn't stop again until the bridge.

But I was wrong.

A few minutes later I hit a patch of rough water. I wasn't worried at all. I'd been through lots worse.

But then the mattress rose up and dumped me into the river.

I don't know what happened. Maybe it was a wave. Or a rock I didn't see. Or the River Demon playing a little joke.

I didn't have time to think about it. Suddenly I was underwater and freezing all over again. The life vest popped me up. I sucked in a breath and realized I was floating along downstream.

The mattress was about six feet ahead of me. I tried to swim toward it, but I couldn't gain much ground. Both the mattress and I drifted along, six feet apart.

Then I hit shallower water. My feet dragged on the bottom. I lifted them high, but soon one foot scraped again. That spun me around.

By then the mattress was fifteen feet ahead. I wanted to scream. I could see it, but I couldn't catch up to it.

All afternoon that mattress had been drifting out of the current. Not now, when I wanted that to happen. Now it sailed along midstream. Getting farther and farther away.

CHAPTER TEN

It was terrible to watch the mattress getting smaller and smaller. I floated along, hoping it would slip out of the current. No such luck.

There was only one thing to do. Obviously. But my brain wasn't working very well. It took me a long time to think of it. Then I paddled and kicked into shallow water. I waded to the shore and started running.

I raced along the water's edge. Up ahead I

could see boulders. If I got that far, I'd have to swim again.

I was almost even with the mattress when it hit some fast water. It shot ahead of me again. I would have screamed if I'd had any breath.

But then the mattress turned sideways for a second. I ran past it and rushed into the river. I kept my eye on the mattress, still upstream from me.

I waded into deeper water. The current pulled at my legs. When I was waist deep, I stopped. I was still wearing my life vest. And it was too late to take it off. If I went any farther, the river would pick me up. And I'd be floating again.

I stopped and watched the mattress come closer. It was moving steadily, right in the middle of the stream. I crouched down and waited.

When the front of the mattress was even with me, I made my leap. I got an arm across the mattress, and it carried me along for a minute. But then it turned sideways, and I eased it toward shore.

I dragged it into shallower water and slid on. I

was still breathing hard from the run, and it felt good to lie down. Even on that mattress.

— — —

On and on I went. I checked my watch about once a minute. Every time I looked ahead, I expected to see the bridge. But all I saw was more river.

I was shivering hard. I tried to make up a song about the bear to keep my mind off the cold. But I couldn't get past the first line:

"On Boulder River I saw a bear. . . ."

I could think of lots of rhymes: *square, fair, hair.* But right then putting words together was too much work.

I gave up the song and started playing games, trying to keep from looking at the watch. I kept my eyes on the water in front of me while I counted to a hundred. Then I glanced at the watch and looked up for the bridge. Then counted again.

I tried to name twenty-five video games I'd played. That didn't work. Right away I started thinking about Tanner.

So I counted backwards from a hundred. And looked up. I counted to five hundred by fives. And looked up. I said the alphabet, then tried to say it backwards.

After counting to ten in Spanish three times, I looked up. And there was the bridge. A plain old metal bridge. But to me, it was beautiful.

I had done it. I'd ridden my crazy mattress-boat all the way. I'd beaten the River Demon.

Paddling toward shore, I kept looking up at that beautiful bridge. Of course, it would have been even more beautiful if people had been standing on it. But I wasn't complaining.

I slid off the mattress and waded to shore. I stripped off my life vest while I ran across the rocks. My sweatshirt, sopping wet, was still tied around my waist. I tried to untie it, but my hands were shaking too hard.

I climbed up the bank to a paved road. I stopped for a second and looked both ways. And saw nothing.

I felt like screaming again. It wasn't fair! I'd come all the way down the river to the bridge. I'd won the game. But there was nothing here. Just an empty road with trees and bushes in both directions.

I glanced down at Tanner's watch and took one long breath. Then I started to run. I chose the left for no reason and raced down the middle of the road. At first, my legs were wobbly. But it still felt good to be moving.

I spotted a metal roof up ahead and ran even faster. Off to the right, down a dirt driveway, was a cabin. Painted white, with a green door. No cars parked in front.

The place looked empty. I ran down the driveway and pounded on that green door anyway.

Nobody there.

I grabbed a rock. I'd use it to break a window. Then I'd climb in and use the phone.

I ran to the first window and looked inside. Bunk beds, an old woodstove. Hanging from the ceiling was an old-fashioned oil lantern.

I groaned and dropped the rock. There wouldn't be a phone in there. They didn't even have electricity.

Just then I heard the rumbling of an engine. What an awesome sound! A truck. Coming this way.

I raced down the driveway. I spotted the truck off to my left. Barreling along. Getting closer and closer.

I couldn't let it get past. This was a race I couldn't lose. I stretched out and ran as hard as I could. Straight into the road.

I stood right in the middle, waving my arms over my head. I heard the horn and squealing brakes. The truck swerved to the edge of the road.

I started to smile. I had won the race. The truck was going to stop.

The squealing brakes got louder. The left head-light was coming right at me. I stood there and watched it get bigger and bigger.

I finally realized that the truck couldn't stop in time. I leapt to the side, and a big fender zipped past me.

The truck screeched to a stop. The air was full of blue smoke from the tires. I rushed forward and slammed my fist against the driver's door.

"You idiot!" the driver shouted. "What's the matter with you?"

"Emergency!" I yelled. "Emergency!"

CHAPTER ELEVEN

The truck driver gave me a jacket and took me to a store with a phone booth on the porch. I called 911. I talked to the operator, then the sheriff's office, then a helicopter pilot from Search and Rescue. When I told him about the yellow X, he laughed and said, "Good job, buddy. This will be a piece of cake."

I dropped the phone and slid down onto the

porch. My legs couldn't hold me any longer. I curled into a ball and closed my eyes.

After that, things get foggy. A woman wrapped me in a blanket and put a bandage on my chin. Somebody gave me hot chocolate, and I spilled it all over the driver's jacket. I spent some time on an old couch, but I can't remember how I got there. I woke up later when Dad was carrying me to the van. "Don't try to talk," he told me. "Tanner's in the hospital. He'll be fine. Just rest."

— — —

Six days later, Tanner was home. He had a bandage on his head, and some of his hair had been shaved. His eyes were purple and puffy. But he still had his puppy-dog smile. Our house was full of balloons and candy. Half the girls in town came by to visit him.

The doctors said Tanner was doing great. But they didn't want him to play football. "That's okay," Tanner said. "I'll try out for the cross-country team." And he'll probably be a star at that, too.

That first night, after his friends finally left, Tanner came to my room. "All right, Ryan," he said, "I want to hear about it."

"What do you mean?"

"I know the way you do things," he said. "You didn't want Mom worrying. So you made it all sound so simple. I want to know what really happened."

"I made up a song about it. You want to hear it?"

"Not really."

"Here's the last verse." I stood up and sang:

"That's my story, and here's the last chapter: I rode a mattress; Tanner, a helicapter."

For once, Tanner didn't smile. "No jokes, Ryan. No dumb songs. I want to hear what happened."

"All right," I said. "But you have to promise not to tell anybody."

"Why not?"

"I don't know. I can't explain it. Just promise me."

"Okay, I promise. Cross my heart and all that stuff. Now, let's hear it."

"We'd better sit down," I said. "It'll take a while."

We sat on my bed, and I told him the whole thing.

When I was done, he shook his head. "I don't get it. What's the big secret? You saved my life twice. First you kept me from drowning. And then you got me rescued. The doctor said I wouldn't have lasted much longer. People ought to know what you did."

"You promised," I said.

"Okay." He got up from the bed. "Wait here a second."

I rested my head on a pillow. I felt better now that Tanner knew the story. I didn't want to tell anybody else right then. I felt good about the whole thing. I'd made mistakes, but I'd done the very best I could. And I was proud of that.

But how could I tell anybody else about it

without seeming to brag? And I didn't want to talk about how lonely and scared I had felt.

Or think about bad things that could have happened.

Tanner came back into the room. He flashed me that same old smile. "I got something for you. And I don't want you acting dumb." He handed me a little white box.

I opened it and looked inside. It was his medal. "No way," I said.

"I told you. Don't be weird about it. I figure you're a real hero, and somebody ought to give you a medal. So that's what I'm doing."

"But it's not—" I started.

"Don't argue with me. Just take it."

Nobody can argue with Tanner. He always gets his way. So I didn't even try.

When Tanner left, I put the medal into the top drawer of my desk. Then I opened another drawer and dug out Chopper Demon.

Just one game before bed. Or, if the Demon zapped me, maybe two.

P. J. Petersen has written many books for young readers. He is a graduate of Stanford University and holds a doctorate in English from the University of New Mexico. He lives with his wife in Redding, California. He has two daughters, Karen and Carly, and two grandchildren, Ryan and Emma.

When he is not writing, P.J. enjoys hiking, kayaking, bicycling, and swimming. When it is raining, he bakes bread, works crossword puzzles, and reads other authors' books.